E
Lyn   Lynam, Terence
           Greg's First Race

Greg's First Race

Special thanks to Gregg Ebertowski and Frank Fuchsberger of Wares Cycle Company, Inc., Milwaukee, for their expert advice, patience, and good humor. Thanks, too, to various helpful people at the Milwaukee Public Library.

THE BMX BUNCH
Greg's First Race   The BMX Bunch Turns Detective
Andy Joins the BMX Bunch   The BMX Bunch on Vacation

Library of Congress Cataloging-in-Publication Data
Lynam, Terence.
   Greg's first race.

   (The BMX Bunch)
   Includes index.
   Summary: Greg enters his first BMX race and meets a
rider who seems very confident.
   [1. Bicycle motocross--Fiction] I. Mostyn, David, ill.
II. Title. III. Series: Lynam, Terence. BMX Bunch.
PZ7.L979737Gr 1988   [E]   87-42816
ISBN 1-55532-440-1
ISBN 1-55532-415-0 (lib. bdg.)

North American edition first published in 1988 by
Gareth Stevens, Inc.
7317 West Green Tree Road
Milwaukee, WI 53223, USA

US edited text and format © 1988 by Gareth Stevens, Inc.
Supplementary text and additional illustrations © l988 by Gareth Stevens, Inc.
Illustrations © 1986 by David Mostyn.

First conceived, edited, designed, and produced in the United Kingdom by Culford Books as *Greg's First Race*, by Terence Lynam, with an original text © 1986 by Culford Books.

Design, this edition: Laurie Shock.
Additional illustrations: Sheri Gibbs.
Series editor: Rhoda Irene Sherwood.
Typeset by Web Tech, Milwaukee.

2 3 4 5 6 7 8 9 93 92 91 90 89 88

Greg's First Race

Terence Lynam
Illustrated by David Mostyn

Gareth Stevens Publishing
Milwaukee

All of the kids in the BMX Bunch were in the park practicing tricks on a slope. Greg and Joe were helping the younger members. As usual, Pete and Jennine were competing to see who was best. Even though he was youngest, Andy was catching on real fast.

"Pretty rad, Andy," said Greg. "Let's show Mom and Dad this one when we get home."

When they were relaxing on the grass, Joe said, "Did you know there's a race Saturday?"

"No," answered Greg. "But I bet I could win." He looked pretty self-confident.

"You *should* enter, Greg," said Andy excitedly. "You could win."

"Yeah," he said thoughtfully. He was moving from self-confident to cocky.

The day before the race, the kids helped Greg get ready. Jennine and Pete oiled the chain. Andy and Joe washed and polished the bike. Greg scrubbed the front wheel. He smiled as he thought about how great he'd look as he pulled ahead in the race.

Saturday morning Greg woke up early. He felt sick.

"It's nerves," his mother said.

"Nerves!" thought Greg. "I'm going to win! Me? Nervous?"

He gathered up his padded jersey, pants, and gloves. He wanted everything to be ready for the race. But his stomach still ached, and he'd lost his helmet.

Even a search in the bathroom and under the kitchen sink didn't turn up his helmet! Greg began to feel frantic. Then he noticed something funny about the cradle his sister Jane had made for her teddy bear!

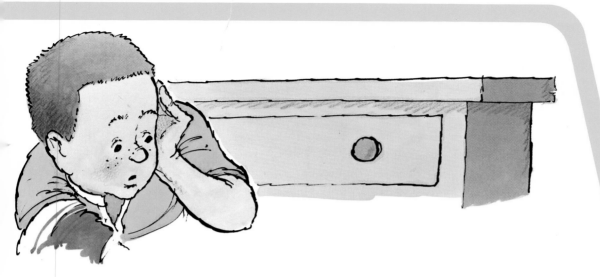

"I'm late!" he cried. "And
you've got my helmet!" Coaxing
it away from her took more time.
Greg was getting more nervous.

13

"Wow," Greg whispered to himself, as the car pulled into the racing area. "I didn't think there'd be so many factory hotshoes here."

15

The BMX Bunch piled out of the Dickinsons' car. They all helped Greg look over his bike again. Jennine and Joe checked the chain and brakes. Pete and Andy felt the tires.

"Look. The front tire's got a flat." Greg felt panicky. "Will you help, Dad?" Mr. Dickinson nodded and went to work. Greg stood by. His stomach flipflopped when he saw that racers had lined up at the starting point.

"Moto 8 to the starting gate," boomed the loudspeaker.

"That's me!" cried Greg. His father had fixed the tire just in time for Greg to race to his place at the gate.

Looking down the course, he forgot his panic. All he saw were the whoops before him. They looked rough. They looked like mountains.

Greg glanced to his right. A tall boy with "Colin the Crazy" splashed across his helmet stood next to a shiny chrome bike.

"He's got a high zoot scoot," Greg thought.

"Hi," Colin said, with a smile. "Is this your first race?"

"Yup," Greg answered, trying to seem casual.

"Ride to the max off the gate, and watch out for Snook's Corner," Colin advised, as he adjusted his helmet.

"What's Snook's . . . ." Greg started to say. Then the gate dropped. They were off.

"Colin just pulled a massive holeshot," Greg thought. "But I'll swoop him at the corner."

Greg heard the roaring crowd. He took the first jump and saw a berm ahead of him.

"Easy," he thought, as he sped down the track. "I'll really crank into this one."

Suddenly, the berm seemed to fly up to meet him. His front wheel slid.

"I'm going to bail," he thought. And seconds later, he did.

"Snook's Corner!" Greg muttered to himself through a mouthful of dirt.

Greg joined the BMX Bunch, just as Colin pulled up. "Did you win?" Greg asked.

"Yeah, I did," said Colin, looking shy but a little proud too. "But you did some aggro riding."

Colin paused. "If you like, I'll meet you later and show you gnarly stuff I've been practicing."

"Great," said Greg. The others agreed.

As he piled into the car with the others, Greg thought, "There's always next year! I can get these tricks wired and do some serious motoing against Colin then. Hm-m-m. I wonder if 'Greg the Gorilla' would fit on my helmet."

BASIC RACING BMX

with rear hand brake only

BMX GEAR

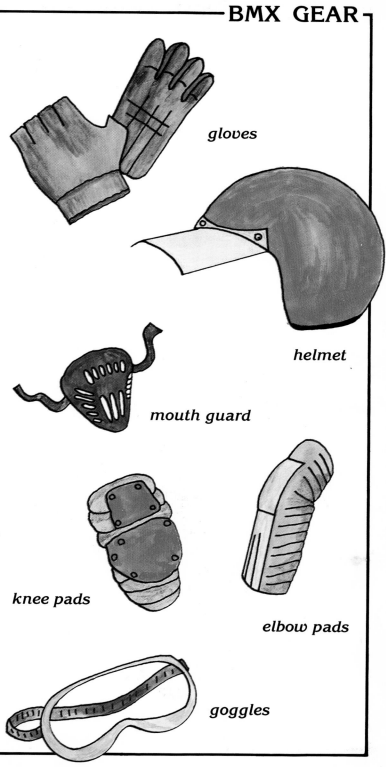

gloves

helmet

mouth guard

knee pads

elbow pads

goggles

27

Safe bikers are rad bikers . . .

Care for Your Bike. Keep your bike in good condition. Check the tires for the right air pressure and for damage done by nails or glass. Tighten loose handlebars, saddle, and spokes. Take your bike to the bike shop to be oiled, greased, and tuned up once a year.

Care for Yourself. When you ride a BMX bike, you should be as careful about yourself and others as you are on any bike. But when you race or do freestyle tricks, you need to be extra careful about protecting yourself from injury. So wear the following protection:

> a padded helmet,
> a mouthguard to protect your nose and teeth,
> goggles to protect your eyes,
> a long-sleeved jersey and pants – padded at the knees and elbows
>   (you may be able to buy pads at your bike store),
> rubber-soled shoes that will grip the pedals,
> sturdy gloves to protect your wrists and hands.

Also have an adult supervise when you practice stunts.

Gnarly rules to know . . .

Follow these basic rules whenever biking in your neighborhood:
1. Obey all traffic signs and other markings on roads.
2. Check with local police about bike rules in your area.
3. Ride single file and on the right side when on the road.
4. Watch for anyone parked on the right who might open a car door.
5. Watch for drain grates, unpaved areas, ruts, and slippery mud.
6. Don't carry passengers or packages that block your view or make it hard for you to handle the bike.
7. Don't ride too close behind trucks or other large vehicles. They will not be able to see you.
8. Wear reflectors at night on your bike and clothing.
9. Be alert at intersections, especially when turning left. Walk your bike in the pedestrian crosswalks at busy intersections.
10. Learn and use these hand signals:

Lots of kids ride bikes these days. The good news is that the percentage of kids being hurt on bikes has dropped since 1940. Good work! You are rad bikers. For information about bicycle safety, write to these addresses:

National Safety Council	Bicycle Forum	Canadian Cycling Association
Bicycle Department	c/o Bike Centennial	333 River Road
444 N. Michigan Avenue	P.O. Box 8308	Vanier, Ontario
Chicago, IL 60611	Missoula, MT 59807	Canada K1L 8H9

Tips for rad racing . . .

Wear all your protective gear. Be sure your bike is in good shape. Practice jumps and turns, and ride to the max when practicing so you know how fast you can go without bailing. At the race:

1. Get a fast start. Keep an eye on the gate and concentrate on the voice of the starter.
2. When the gate goes down, really crank to the first obstacle.
3. If you get to corners first, take the inside position. If other racers get there first, look for an open lane so you can swoop them. On banked turns, put the inside foot down and drag it lightly on the ground to balance yourself.
4. To jump whoops, crank going into them, shift your weight to the back and pull the front wheel up, use your pedals to brace yourself for the landing, come down on your rear wheel, and then shift your weight to the front again so your front tire comes down. Get off jumps as fast as you can! Time spent in the air is time wasted!

Don't be a squid! Show good manners: In the heat of the race, hold your ground, but don't be overly aggro if you can help it, or you'll be thrown out for bad sportsmanship. As BMX racers say, "Go for it and ride to the max. Don't worry that you're not as smooth as others. Get out and try."

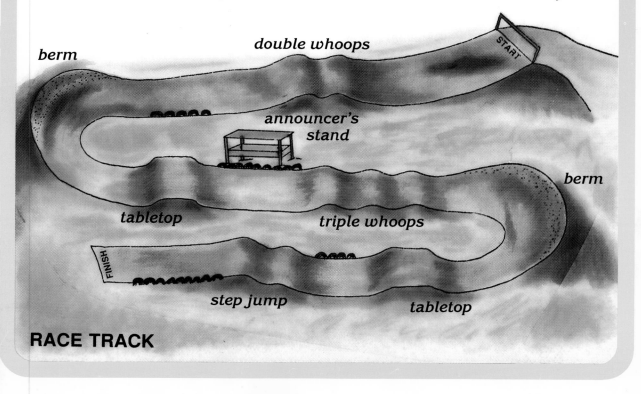

RACE TRACK

MORE ABOUT BMX . . .

Clubs

These clubs hold BMX races and freestyle shows throughout the US and Canada. Write to them if you are interested in their races, prizes, and other awards. BMX racing is so popular, these clubs are moving to get it into the Olympics. Also call your local bike shop to find out about shows and classes in your area for kids interested in freestyling and racing.

National Bicycle League (NBL)
555 Metro Place North, Suite 524
Dublin, OH 43017

American Bicycle Association (ABA)
6501 W. Frye Road
Chandler, AZ 85226

American Freestyle Association (AFA)
P.O. Box 2339
Cyprus, CA 90630

Canadian-American Bicycling Association (CABA)
6520 82nd Avenue, 2nd Floor
Edmonton, Alberta
Canada   T6B 0E7

Books

If you'd like to read more about BMX bikes, freestyling, and racing, see if your local library, bookstore, or bike store have the following:

BMX: A Guide to Bicycle Motocross. Coombs (Morrow)
BMX! Bicycle Motocross for Beginners. Edmonds (Holt, Rinehart & Winston)
Better BMX Riding and Racing for Boys and Girls. Sullivan (Dodd)

And for more books about the BMX Bunch, read

Andy Joins the BMX Bunch
The BMX Bunch Turns Detective
The BMX Bunch on Vacation

Magazines

Check your local library to see if they have these magazines. To subscribe to them, write to the publishers at the addresses listed below:

American BMX-er
...in the States:
American Bicycle Association
P.O. Box 718
Chandler, AZ 85244

BMX Action and *Freestylin'*
Wizard Publications, Inc.
3162 Kashiwa Street
Torrance, CA 90505

Bicycles Today
National Bicycle League
555 Metro Place North, Suite 524
Dublin, OH 43017

American BMX-er
... in Canada:
Canadian-American Bicycling Association
6520 82nd Avenue, 2nd Floor
Edmonton, Alberta
Canada   T6B 0E7

Super BMX and Freestyle
Challenge Publications, Inc.
7950 Deering Avenue
Canoga Park, CA 91304

BMX Plus
1760 Kaiser Avenue
Irvine, CA 92714

Also check to see if your local video store has the BMX video called RAD. It's directed by Hal Needham and made by Talia Films II, Ltd.

GLOSSARY OF NEW WORDS — Here are some words you may not know and the pages where you can find them. Some of these words are used by many people; others are used by BMX-ers. After each word is explained, it is used in a sentence.